THIS WALKER BOOK BELONGS TO:

_____

_____

_____

To Bob and Margaret ⌁ J.E.
For Millie ⌁ V.C.

First published 2006 by Walker Books Ltd
87 Vauxhall Walk, London SE11 5HJ

4 6 8 10 9 7 5 3

Text © 2006 Jonathan Emmett
Illustrations © 2006 Vanessa Cabban

The right of Jonathan Emmett and Vanessa Cabban to be identified
as author and illustrator respectively of this work has been asserted by
them in accordance with the Copyright, Designs and Patents Act 1988

You can find out more about Jonathan Emmett's books
by visiting his website at www.scribblestreet.co.uk

This book has been typeset in Beta Bold

Printed in China

British Library Cataloguing in Publication Data: a catalogue record
for this book is available from the British Library.

ISBN 978-1-4063-0596-8

www.walker.co.uk

# Diamond
## in the
# Snow

Jonathan Emmett

illustrated by Vanessa Cabban

WALKER BOOKS
AND SUBSIDIARIES

LONDON · BOSTON · SYDNEY · AUCKLAND

"COLD-diggerty!" gasped Mole,
as he burrowed out
of the ground one afternoon.
"Whatever's this?"

It was the middle of winter
and the woodland was covered
in a thick blanket
of snow.

Mole had never seen snow before.

It made the woodland look strange and beautiful.

So Mole left his hole and set off to explore.

It was SO quiet, as if everything

had fallen under a magic spell.

Mole wandered on, enchanted,

until suddenly ...

he found
   himself sliding
down a steep,
      snowy bank.

"Ooh!"
cried Mole,
as his paws slipped
from under him.

**"Wheee!"**
he shouted,
as he sped down
the slope.

**"Ooooofff!"**
he groaned,
as he crashed into
a tree trunk.

Mole picked himself
up – and then gasped
with surprise.
Something smooth
and sparkly was sticking out
of the snow beside him.
Mole was sure that it hadn't been
there a moment ago.

"It's as if it appeared by MAGIC," thought Mole.
"It looks like a diamond," he decided.
"I must take it home!"

Mole carried
the diamond back
up the steep bank.
It was hard work.
The diamond had
become wet
  and slippery
and was
  very difficult
    to hold.

"Drat!"
  said Mole,
  as he stumbled
  and the
    diamond
  shot up
  out of his
    paws.

"It's as
if it were
trying to escape,"
gasped Mole, as he
chased it down
the slope.

"Perhaps it's
a MAGIC diamond,"
he thought.

"Phew!" panted Mole,
when he finally reached the top
of the bank. He was HOT and tired,
but he hurried on, anxious to get home.
By now, he was sure that the diamond
was magical, because it was changing shape
in his paws.

He was almost home, when he suddenly
realized that his arms were empty.
The diamond had disappeared
                    – right from under his nose!

Just then a snowball
came whizzing through the air,
closely followed by Hedgehog,
Squirrel and Rabbit.

"Hello, Mole," said Hedgehog, cheerily.

"Do you want to come snowballing with us?"
asked Squirrel.

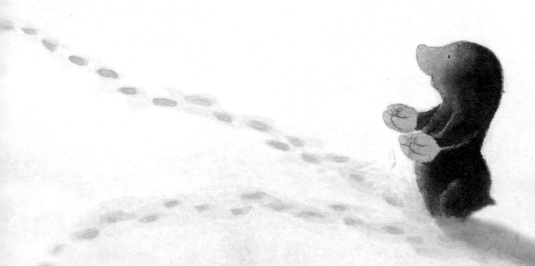

But Mole was still staring unhappily
at his empty paws.

"What's wrong, Mole?"
asked Rabbit.

So Mole told them
all about the magic diamond
– how it had appeared from nowhere,
and changed shape and tried to escape
– and how it had finally disappeared
from under his nose.

But Mole could tell that his friends
didn't really believe him. So he took
them back to the tree trunk
where the diamond had first appeared.

"That's where I found it," said Mole,
pointing DOWN into the snow.
Rabbit, Hedgehog and Squirrel
were all smiling.

"Look," said Rabbit,
pointing UP into the tree.
Mole squinted up – and then he saw them!
The tree above them was filled with
HUNDREDS of diamonds.
They were hanging from every branch.

"They're ICICLES," said Squirrel.

"They're just frozen water," said Hedgehog.

"The one you found must have melted
in your paws," explained Rabbit.

"So it wasn't magic then,"
said Mole, sadly.

"Not really,"
said Rabbit, kindly.

The four friends set off
up the bank again. But when they got
to the top, Mole glanced back to take
one last look at the icicle tree.

"Wait a minute,"
he said excitedly. "LOOK!"

The sun was setting
over the snowy woodland,
casting its last rays into the branches
of the tree, making each icicle shimmer
with a beautiful golden light.
It was the most SPECTACULAR thing
that any of them had ever seen.

Mole, Rabbit, Hedgehog and Squirrel stood
staring at the tree, enchanted, until the last
of the light had died away.

"That was MARVELLOUS,"
sighed Rabbit, as they made their way
back through the woodland.

"WONDERFUL," agreed Hedgehog.

"FANTASTIC," added Squirrel.

"You see," said Mole, grinning proudly.
  "I told you they were
    MAGIC!"

WALKER BOOKS is the world's leading

independent publisher of children's books.

Working with the best authors and illustrators

we create books for all ages, from babies

to teenagers – books your child will

grow up with and always remember. So…

FOR THE BEST CHILDREN'S BOOKS,
LOOK FOR THE BEAR